GET WELL, SANTA!

ORIGINALLY PUBLISHED AS *BLESS YOU, SANTA!*

For Georgia, Isabel and Victoria
—*JS*

For Jane—howdy pardner!
—*TW*

ISBN 0-439-72987-4

Text copyright © 2004 by Julie Sykes. Illustrations copyright © 2004
by Tim Warnes. Originally published as *Bless You, Santa!* All rights
reserved. Published by Scholastic Inc., 557 Broadway,
New York, NY 10012, by arrangement with Tiger Tales,
an imprint of ME Media LLC. SCHOLASTIC and associated logos
are trademarks and/or registered trademarks of Scholastic Inc.

12 11 10 9 8 7 6 5 4 3 2 1   4 5 6 7 8 9/0

Printed in the U.S.A.   40

First Scholastic printing, November 2004

GET WELL, SANTA!

ORIGINALLY PUBLISHED AS *BLESS YOU, SANTA!*

by Julie Sykes

Illustrated by Tim Warnes

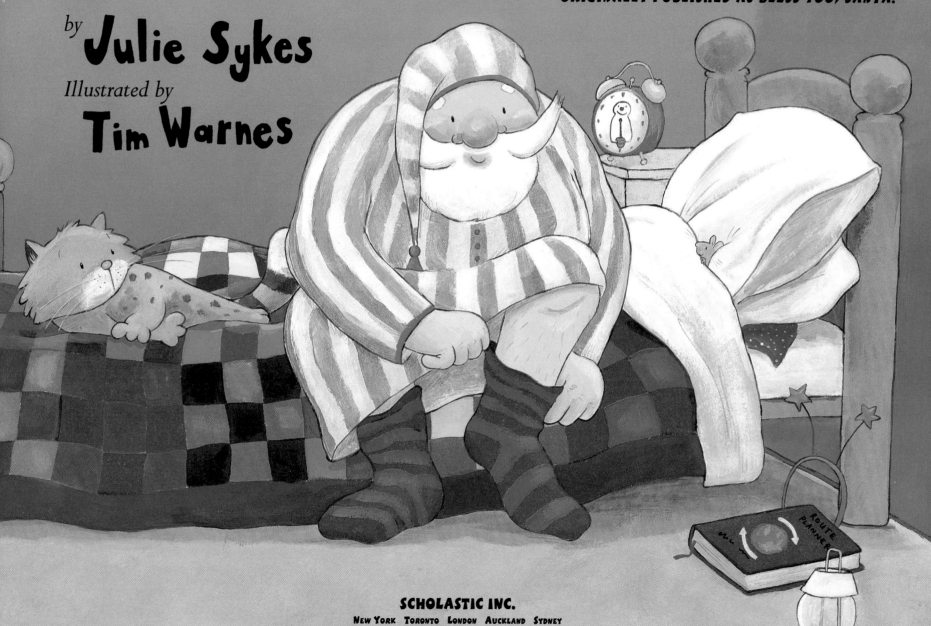

SCHOLASTIC INC.

NEW YORK   TORONTO   LONDON   AUCKLAND   SYDNEY
MEXICO CITY   NEW DELHI   HONG KONG   BUENOS AIRES

It was almost Christmas, and Santa was up very early one day.

"Jingle bells, jingle bells," he sang to himself. "Breakfast first and then to work."

He made some toast and took out the jam and butter. As he was pouring some cereal, though, his nose began to tickle.

"Aah, aah, aah . . ."

DECEMBER
23

"ACHOOOo!"

he roared. His sneeze blew
the cereal all over the place!

"Bless you, Santa," said Santa's cat, shaking
cereal out of her tail. "That's a nasty cold."
"Oh, no!" said Santa in alarm. "It can't be.
It's nearly Christmas. I don't have time for a cold."

After breakfast Santa rushed to his workshop
and went to work on the unfinished toys. Happily
he sang as he painted a robot. But Santa's sneezes
were growing larger and louder.
"Aah, aah, aah . . ."

"ACHOOOO!"

"Bless you, Santa," squeaked Santa's little mouse, gathering the beads his sneeze had scattered across the table.

"Bless you, Santa," said Santa's cat, chasing paper stars as they fluttered around. "You sound awful. Go and sit by the fire."

"I feel awful," said Santa. "But I can't rest yet. It's too close to Christmas. I have to finish these toys or there will be no presents for all the . . . aah, aah, aah . . ."

"ACHOOOo!"

Santa sneezed so hard that he slipped and landed in a pile of balls. Down the balls tumbled, bouncing off Santa and bouncing around the room. They crashed into cars, they pushed over paint cans, they toppled the teddy bears, and they ruined the rockets.

"ACHOOOo!"

"Just look at this mess!" cried Santa. "I'll never by ready in time for Christmas."

"Go to bed, Santa," ordered his little mouse. "You're not well. Your nose is so red the reindeer could use it to guide your sleigh. We'll clean up this mess and get everything ready for Christmas."

So Santa's mouse put Santa to bed with a mug of hot tea and a little medicine to help his cold.

Santa snuggled into the blanket.

He sneezed. "ACHOOOO!"

He sniffled.

And finally he snored.

sssh!

zzzzzzZZZZZZZ ZZZZ Z Z ZZZZZZZZZZZZ

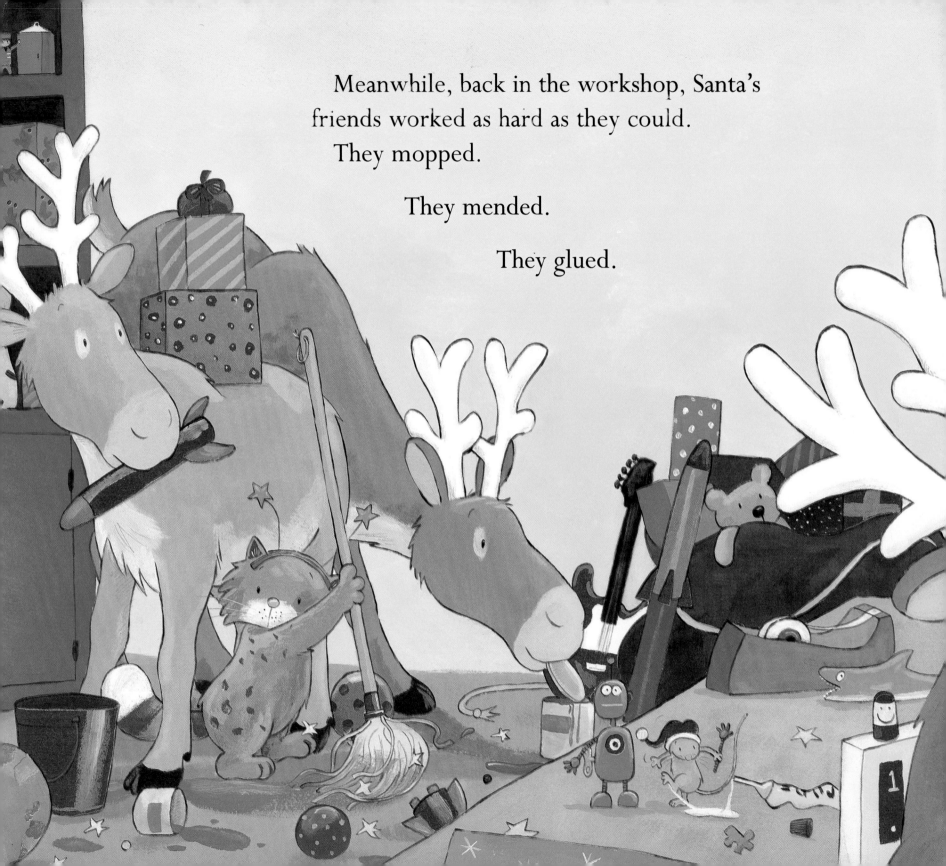

Meanwhile, back in the workshop, Santa's
friends worked as hard as they could.
They mopped.

They mended.

They glued.

They snipped, they stuck, and they
wrapped. Faster and faster they worked
until every single present was finished.
Then sleepily they went to bed.

The next evening, as the sun set, the animals waited with the sleigh piled high with toys.

"Where is Santa?" asked Santa's cat. "I hope he's better."

"Who's going to drive the sleigh and deliver all the presents?" asked the reindeer.

"Listen," said Santa's cat. "Can you hear something?"

The animals listened.

"It's Santa!" squeaked Santa's little mouse. "Are you better, Santa? Can you deliver the presents?"
Santa wrinkled his nose.
"Aah, aah, aah . . ."

"Ho, ho, ho!" chuckled Santa loudly.

"Only joking! I feel much better. Bless you,
everyone. You did a great job! Thanks to you
I will get these presents delivered in time for
Christmas morning."

Santa climbed aboard his sleigh. "Reindeer,
up, up, and away!" he shouted.

It was a busy night as Santa flew
around the world delivering presents.

When at last Santa landed back at the
North Pole the sun was rising. But he hadn't
finished quite yet.

"These presents are for you," said Santa.

"Presents for us?" squeaked Santa's cat.
"Th . . . th . . . thaa . . ."

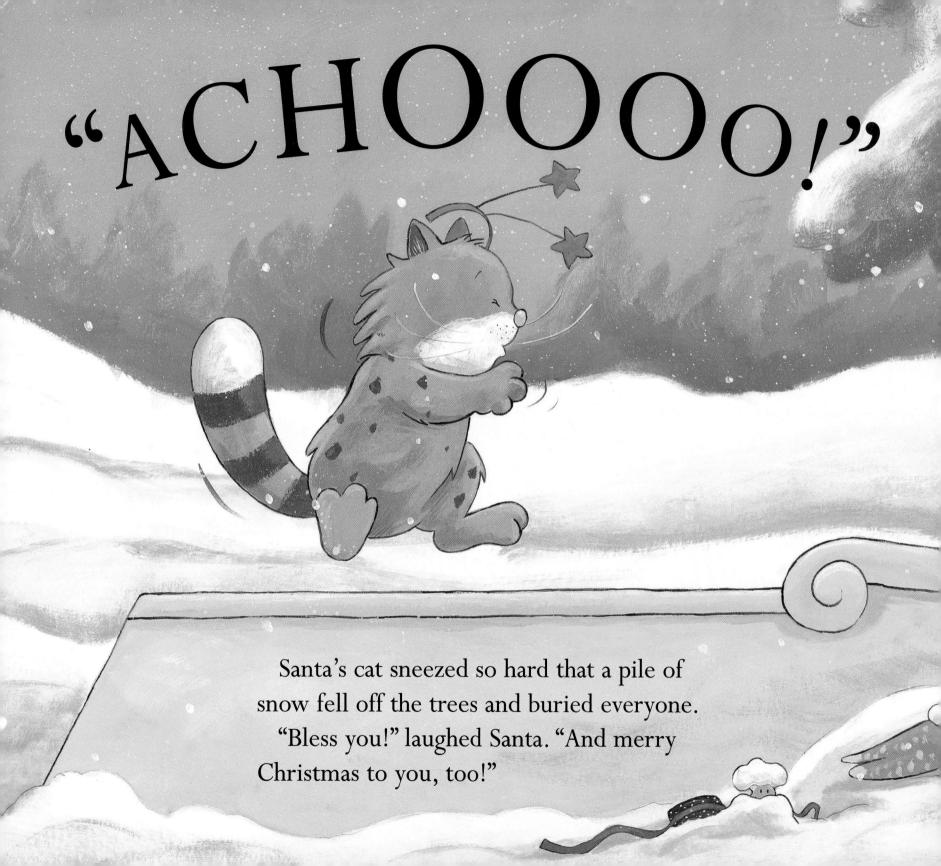

"ACHOOOo!"

Santa's cat sneezed so hard that a pile of
snow fell off the trees and buried everyone.
"Bless you!" laughed Santa. "And merry
Christmas to you, too!"